For Rilynne

A thank-you song to Christy Ottaviano
to be sung to a tune by The Commodores:

(Chorus)
She's a WORD–HOUSE!
Re-write, re-write me, she takes all my bad words out.
She's a WORD–HOUSE!
Her brain is stacked with lots of facts.
She's nice and she has no plaque.

(Bridge)
She knows nouns, she knows nouns, she knows nouns now. *(Repeat)*

* * *

Thanks, Mom, Scott, and Joan, for your
continuous support and encouragement.

Do Unto Otters by Laurie Keller. Copyright © 2007 by Laurie Keller.
Reprinted by permission of Henry Holt Books for Young Readers.

Houghton Mifflin Harcourt Edition

Printed in Mexico
ISBN   978-1-328-52306-8

1 2 3 4 5 6 7 8 9 10   0908   27 26 25 24 23 22 21 20 19 18

4500719364   A B C D E F G

Hi, Hilde!

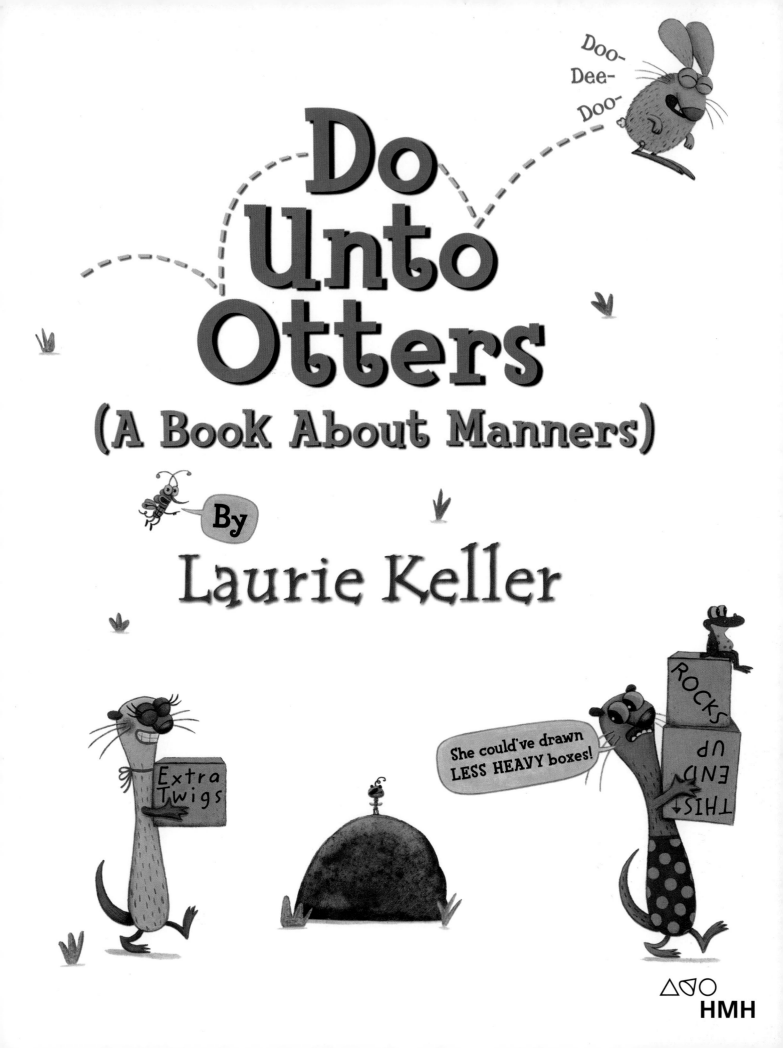

DOO-
DEE-
DOO

DOO-
DEE-
DOO

DOO-DEE-DOO

DOO-
DEE-
DOO

back home

3

Hello, Mr. Rabbit.
We're your new neighbors,
the OTTERS!

I don't know anything about <u>otters</u>. What if we don't get along?

Mr. Rabbit, I know an old saying:

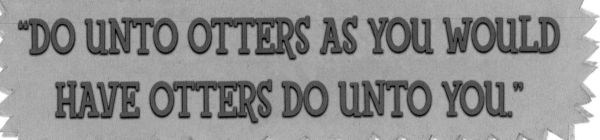

"DO UNTO OTTERS AS YOU WOULD HAVE OTTERS DO UNTO YOU."

What does **THAT** mean?

It simply means treat otters the same way you'd like otters to treat you.

Treat otters the same way I'd like otters to treat me?

Hmmm...

How would I like otters to treat me?

8

How would I...

...like OTTERS...

...to treat ME?

Well . . . I'd like otters to be FRIENDLY.

A cheerful hello,

Howdy, neighbor!

a nice smile,

and good eye contact

Blah blah blah . . .

are all part of being friendly.

Friendliness is very important to me—especially after my last neighbor, Mrs. Grrrrrr.

I'd like otters to be POLITE.

They should know when to say

"PLEASE."

PLEASE LOOK

Yoohoo, Mr. Rabbit... would you please return my ball there? PRETTY PLEASE with CARROTS on top?
Would you like me to stop stinging you?
Yes, PLEASE.
Hee hee . . . carrots
I can say "PLEASE" in 5 languages:
"Por Favor" (Spanish)
"S'il vous plaît" (French)
"Bitte" (German)
"Kudasai" (Japanese)
"Easeplay" (Pig Latin)
Impressive!
Say the "MAGIC WORD" and I'll turn these clams into a MILLION DOLLARS!
Magic word rhymes with this.

They should know when to say

"THANK YOU."

THANKS FOR LOOKING! C:

Dear Mr. Rabbit,
Thank you very much
for returning my ball.
You must have returned
a lot of balls before
because you made it
look so easy! Balls sure
are bouncy and roll-y
but I'LL try to keep it
under control next time.
Sincerely,

Would you like me to sting you now?

NO, thank you.

Then please take my BEE-zness card and call me when you're ready.

Nice beak.

Thanks!

I can say "THANK YOU" in ⑤ languages:

"Gracias" (Spanish)

"Merci" (French)

"Danke schön" (German)

"Arigato" (Japanese)

"Ankthay ouyay" (Pig Latin)

Superb!

Did you say "PLEASE" or "CHEESE"?

And they should know when to say

"EXCUSE ME."

EXCUSE ME!
BURP

16

EXCUSE ME!!

Excuse me, Mr. Bee, I need to run and check on something...

OOPS!

I can say **"EXCUSE ME"** in ⑤ languages:

"Dispénserne" (Spanish)

"Pardonnez-moi" (French)

"Entschuldigen Sie" (German)

"Sumimasen" (Japanese)

"Excuseway emay" (Pig Latin)

Well, "P–U" is the same in ANY language!

Pffft!

Hmm... it worked in rehearsal.

Excuse me for interrupting your reading, but I heard you say "PLEASE," not "CHEESE."

Otters should be
HONEST.

18

That means they should

KEEP THEIR PROMISES

NOT LIE

NOT CHEAT

I'd like otters to be **CONSIDERATE**.

20

You know...

It's always good to have a considerate neighbor.

It wouldn't hurt otters to be KIND.

(Everyone appreciates a kind act
no matter how bad it smells.)

Oh, and what's that word?...

"COOPERATE!"

Otters should learn to cooperate.

Did someone say "OPERATE"?

CO-operate: to work well together

We know how to co-OTTER-ate!

I see otters
like to play.

Wheeeeee!

I hope they Know how to **PLAY FAIR.**

Come on, you two!

You won!

OTTERS' RULES FOR FAIR PLAY

Be a GOOD SPORT

Play by the rules

Take turns

Include EVERYONE

(even BEES)

I'd like it
if we could
SHARE
things:

our favorite books,

Harry Otter

Goldilocks
and the
Three
Hares

our favorite activities,

our favorite treats

(hmmm ... maybe not the treats).

I hope otters WON'T TEASE me about:

My "Doo-Dee-Doo" song

My extra-large swim fins

My "bad hare days"

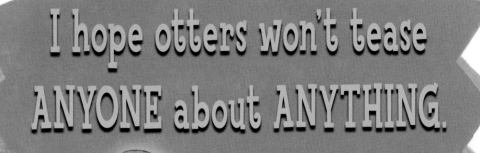

I hope otters won't tease ANYONE about ANYTHING.

Teasing is MEAN.

It's the WORST!

It's worse than having a clam snap shut on your nose!

I think otters should APOLOGIZE when they do something wrong.

30

And I hope they can be **FORGIVING** when I do something wrong.

So there.
That's how I'd
like otters to
treat me.

You see,
Mr. Rabbit,
I told you it
was simple!

DOO-
DEE-
DOO

DOO-
DEE-
DOO

DOO-
DEE-
DOO

Mr.
Rabbit's
House

Home
Sweet
Home

RIGHT! Just
"DOO-DEE-DOO
unto otters as you
would have otters

unto you!"